# THE  MILLS & BOON®
## Centenary Collection

**Celebrating 100 years of romance with
the very best of Mills & Boon**

First published in Great Britain 2008
by Harlequin Mills & Boon Limited,
Eton House, 18-24 Paradise Road, Richmond, Surrey TW9 1SR

© Penny Jordan 1999

ISBN: 978 0 263 86613 1

76-0208

Harlequin Mills & Boon policy is to use papers that are
natural, renewable and recyclable products and made from
wood grown in sustainable forests. The logging and
manufacturing processes conform to the legal environmental
regulations of the country of origin.

Printed and bound in Spain
by Litografia Rosés S.A., Barcelona

# They're Wed Again

by
Penny Jordan

MILLS & BOON
*Pure reading pleasure*

**Penny Jordan** has been writing for more than twenty years and has an outstanding record: over one hundred and thirty novels published, including the phenomenally successful *A Perfect Family, To Love, Honour & Betray, The Perfect Sinner* and *Power Play* which hit *The Sunday Times* and *New York Times* bestseller lists. Penny Jordan was born in Preston, Lancashire, and now lives in rural Cheshire.

One of Mills & Boon's best-loved writers, Penny writes for the Modern™ series and contributes to M&B™. Look out for the continuation of her Arabian Nights series in Modern in June and the return of the Creightons in M&B in May and June!

# CHAPTER ONE

'AUNT BELLE! You look *wonderful*, positively glowing…'

'Shouldn't that be *my* line to *you*?' Isabelle smiled as she hugged her newly married niece, and then stepped back to admire her wedding dress.

'I'm sorry about the mix-up with the invitations,' Joy apologised. 'But Great-Aunt Alice insisted on helping Mum to write them, and you *know* what she's like.' She pulled a wry face. 'She completely forgot that you and Luscious Lucius got divorced simply ages ago, and sent you both joint invitations to his address…'

'"Luscious Lucius." You still call him that, do you?' Isabelle teased her niece, smiling a warm look at Joy's new husband.

'Oh, Andy doesn't mind,' Joy laughed back. 'After all, Luc *is* his cousin, and besides—' she gave her new husband a mock stern look '—Andy has always thought that *you* are gorgeously sexy—for an older woman…'

As the groom went pink, and tugged at his cravat, Isabelle raised her eyebrows. She was thirty-four, almost thirty-five, to Joy's twenty-three—not yet in her dotage, surely?

At Joy's age she and Luc had already been married for close on two years. They had married far too immature—a girl whom marriage had hot-housed into a woman. And while Luc might have loved the girl he had married, he had certainly ceased to love the woman that girl had become.

As she had told Luc at the time, she'd thought it grossly unfair that he had refused to acknowledge and appreciate the stresses that her career had placed on her, the anxiety that being the main breadwinner in their household had caused her. And then, on top of that anxiety, to have Luc complain that she was never at home, that she valued her job more than she did him, had been just too much for her to endure, and had ultimately caused the series of destructive rows which had eventually led to their divorce.

'Luc, I have hardly any time to myself,' she had pointed out to him during one of their arguments. 'When I *am* at home, I have housework to do, food to buy—this house doesn't clean itself, you know. I'm the one who has to worry about paying the mortgage and keeping the cupboards filled—all you have to worry about is your precious studying. Sometimes I think that is all you do think about—care about!'

Belle could still remember how his face had darkened, his eyes clouding as he'd turned away from her, his head seeming to hang a little. At over six foot he was much, much taller than her, but as he'd moved away from her then he'd looked oddly shrunken and defeated, humiliated and humbled somehow, and along with her anger she had felt a sense of anguish and pain, a sharp flash of panic which she'd quickly pushed to one side.

If she had thought about the subject at all before they had married, she had assumed naively that their marriage would be an idyll, a continuation of the hours, and days, and the very occasional stolen weekends they had managed to snatch since their first meeting earlier in the year when she, newly graduated and working for the high-powered city firm of financial analysts where she had been lucky to get a job, had been introduced by a friend to the brilliant young mathematician who had turned his back on the profitable world of commerce and finance and who, idealistically, had opted instead to devote himself to further study and ultimately a career as a university lecturer.

It had been a private joke between them in those early days that she was the one with the large salary and the company car, whilst he was the one still eking out a meagre living on a grant. But there had been no doubt in Belle's mind about her feelings, her love for Luc, and she had admired him intensely for his dedication and his idealism.

'I want to marry you...' Luc had told her longingly a few months into their courtship. 'I want us to be together for always. But I can barely afford to support myself, never mind a wife...'

'We could live on my salary,' Belle had told him sunnily, far too deeply in love with him to care how they financed their lives, just as long as they shared them.

If anyone had warned her then that her job, her earnings, which had made it possible for them to be together, would one day be the cause of them breaking up, she would have laughed in immediate denial. Her love for Luc and his love for her had been so strong, so meant by fate, that she'd been sure nothing could ever make them part.

\* \* \*

She might have been in the vanguard of a movement that had women taking on a much more prominent role in financing their own and their partner's lives, but striking a blow for equality had been the last thing on Belle's mind when, a few years into their marriage, she had persuaded Luc that it made more sense for them to buy a house now that they were married than for her to go on sharing his cramped rented accommodation. They could afford the mortgage after all. She had just been promoted and had received a good rise.

'You mean *you* can afford it,' Luc had corrected her gently, but Belle hadn't really heard him. She had been far too busy excitedly studying the house details she had brought home with her, dreaming already of how she would decorate their new home.

And in the end Luc had gone along with her wishes, and they had bought the pretty village property they had both fallen for in the small, and in those days undeveloped village within reasonably easy commuting distance of London and close to Cambridge, where Luc eventually hoped to get a university post.

'I won't be able to use my bike to get to college any more,' Luc had protested when they had first gone to see the house.

'You can travel by train, like I do,' Belle had pointed out. 'We can travel to the station together in my car.'

'What about the days when you leave at six and don't get back until nine or ten?' Luc had reminded her, but Belle had been so desperately in love with the house, so sure it was perfect for them, that eventually he had given way—as she had known he would.

They had celebrated their first night of owning the house in the big double bedroom in front of the fireplace, lying on their duvet on the bare floorboards. Luc, always romantic, had insisted on lighting a fire in the hearth, and the room had smelled of woodsmoke and candles. There had been a problem getting the electricity turned on, Belle remembered, and she had gone to try to sort it out. In her absence Luc had been out and bought candles—hundreds of them, or so it had seemed. They had lit her way up the stairs where Luc had carefully and formally ushered her into their bedroom.

In their soft glow Luc's face had taken on a sternness, a maturity which had both startled her a little and thrilled her. She'd become so used to his gentle, easygoing acceptance of whatever plans she made, that to see him looking so purposeful and determined had touched a little feminine nerve inside her that had made her ache with longing for him.

'This house is our home,' Luc told her as he started to undress her. 'Our home, Belle. We'll work on it, shape it, share in it together… I know it's *your* salary that's made it possible for us to buy it, but it takes more than money to make a home, and I want our home to be something we've *both* worked for…'

There was a warning there for her to heed, but she neglected to do so, shivering a little in the cool evening air, despite the warmth of Luc's smoky fire, snuggling up close to him as he removed the last of their clothing, opening her mouth eagerly to the hungry passion of his as he started to kiss her.

The physical attraction between them had been immediate and intense right from the start; Luc, three, nearly four years her senior, had technically at least been the more experienced of the two of them, but, as he had freely and adoringly admitted to Belle, she had brought to their relationship and to him a sexual intensity and an emotional openness that made him feel that everything he had experienced before, everything he had thought he knew, had been merely a pale shadow of their shared reality.

Now, with their kisses growing deeper and deeper, and the warm, silk-rough glide of Luc's hands over her eager body, Belle forgot how cold it was, how cheerless the empty, unfurnished room; she forgot, too, the hassle she had had over their unconnected electricity supply, the irritation she had experienced with Luc because he had been so engrossed in his studies that he had forgotten to notify the authorities in time to have the supply reconnected before they moved in. What did that kind of electricity matter when the variety *they* created between them was so intense that it could fuel a whole universe?

The duvet was soft and inviting, even if at the back of Belle's mind lay the knowledge that it would have to be washed before it could go anywhere near the new bed she intended to persuade Luc to agree to her buying; the glow from the candles was doing wonderful things to the soft curves of her body and Luc's, and the glow in Luc's eyes was making her burn so hotly for him that her tremulous, almost panting breath was threatening to blow those candles closest to them out.

'Luc…'

Wantonly she reached for him, pressing her open mouth to each hollow and curve of his candlelight-shadowed body, feeling him tense and shudder in wild reaction to her sensuous caresses.

Her tongue-tip teased the dark arrowing of hair that spread with delicious invitation down the length of his torso, a rich, fertile valley all excitingly male, yielding a harvest that Belle already knew full well more than lived up to its promise. There was an idealistic intensity about Luc that he brought to everything he did, but most especially to his love for her.

She was his first real true love. He had once told her in the early days of their relationship that she would always be his one true love.

Belle loved him just as intensely, but there was a practicality about her nature which made her sometimes feel just a little impatient of Luc's idealism and his total lack of interest in anything material.

Of course, like him, she agreed that no amount of money or material possessions could make up for a lack of love; that what they had, what they *shared*, was worth more than a king's ransom, a hundred kings' ransoms, but… But just think how wonderful it would have been tonight if they had been making love in their new bed, the handsome king-sized one she had seen in the small exclusive handmade furniture shop just outside Cambridge, a bed with a wonderful hand-carved headboard. They could have their initials carved into it, and some special symbol to represent their love…

And then, as Luc's tenderly roving hands touched those most secret, sacred places of her body, she forgot all about the new bed and the mess the dusty floor would be making of their duvet, as a small moan of blissful pleasure escaped her lips.

She remembered about it the following day, though, as she complained to Luc about the dust-marks on the duvet and the candle wax that had fallen on it.

'It's a duvet—a piece of fabric. It will wash,' Luc had defended.

'Oh, yes, it will wash,' Belle agreed, tight-lipped. 'But not here and not by me. For one thing we don't possess a washing machine, and for another, even if we did, we don't have any elec-tricity supply to run it.'

'Look, I'm sorry about that. I've already ex-plained, Professor Lind wanted to ask my opinion about…'

Professor Lind was something of an idol to Luc, who desperately wanted to emulate the older man's academic achievements. Belle had met him several times but sensed that, like Luc, he was rather contemptuous of her much more materially based world. She also rather suspected that the professor felt Luc had made a mistake in marrying her, and when she had taxed Luc with this he had looked a little embarrassed and finally admitted that the professor *had* counselled him against getting married.

'He doesn't think any man should get married until he's over thirty,' he had told Belle ruefully, adding huskily, 'But then he's obviously never met a woman like you…never been in love…'

Discussing the duvet reminded Belle of the bed she had seen but, predictably, Luc objected the moment she had told him where she had seen it.

'It will be far too expensive for us,' he told her, his voice suddenly unusually curt and hard.

'Oh, Luc…I want us to have something special, passed on not from either of our parents, something that's ours…' she told him softly, moving towards him, intending to snuggle into his arms.

But to her chagrin he turned away from her, his face unexpectedly grim as he told her sharply, 'I thought we already had something special.'

'The house…' Belle agreed. 'Oh, yes, but I want it to be furnished as specially as it deserves, and—'

'No, Belle, *not* the house,' Luc told her distantly. 'I was referring to our love itself…'

\* \* \*

They made up the quarrel on that occasion, but the issue of the new bed remained unresolved—until Belle thought she had found an ideal way of circumventing it.

Christmas was less than six weeks away, and the bed she coveted was tantalisingly on display in the small Cambridgeshire store where she had first viewed it.

One night, after they had made love and then were lying sensually entwined in the cramped space of the old three-quarter bed Luc's parents had given them, Belle tentatively raised the subject of a new bed again.

'I really loved that one I told you about,' she told Luc softly. 'And it would look wonderful here in this house…this room…'

Their house was old, eighteenth century and cottagey, and it cried out for sturdy, hand-made proper furniture, but of course such furniture was expensive.

'It would make a wonderful Christmas present to ourselves,' she wheedled softly in Luc's ear. He had proved increasingly stubborn of late about her contribution to their household, refusing to allow her to spend her unexpectedly high bonus on furniture, telling her that it was her money—not theirs.

'Don't you understand…? Can't you see…?

I've seen the look on the faces of your friends, your family, when they come round here. They know there's no way *we* could afford to live somewhere like this, to buy a house like this, whilst *I'm* still virtually having to live on a grant…'

'You earn extra from the private tuition you give,' Belle protested.

Luc gave a harsh laugh.

'*Extra!* A pittance…*peanuts* compared to what you're earning. Look, I know what you're saying about the bed, and I do understand… But Belle, please, just this once, please indulge me. There's something… Trust me, Belle.'

'Well, if you insist,' Belle agreed, but secretly she was already planning to surprise him on Christmas Eve with the delivery of the new bed and the headboard. She would tell him that it was a present to both of them—which it was, of course. And he would understand. She knew he would.

When she went in to order the bed a week later, she soothed her conscience by telling herself that it was just silly male pride that was making Luc so difficult over it, and that he would soon forget all about his veto once he had seen how beautifully it suited the house.

At work the run-up to Christmas was hectic, a

frenetic mixture of deadlines and glittery, no-expenses-spared client parties.

In Cambridge Luc's college was empty of students for the Christmas break, enabling Luc to take full advantage of the college library and its other facilities for his own studies. But in order to help out with the mortgage he had taken on more and more private tuition, leaving him less and less time for his own work.

'Pure maths at Luc's level requires a devotion and commitment which is almost on a par with that once required by the priesthood,' Luc's mentor told Belle severely when she gave in to Luc's quiet insistence and accompanied him to Professor Lind's pre-Christmas drinks party—a sedate affair, held in the chilly monastic starkness of his college rooms, the only food and drink on offer his housekeeper's home-made and deeply unpleasant mince pies and a sherry which made Belle grit her teeth.

'You know I only drink champagne,' she told Luc plaintively. After the luxury of vintage champagne and the delicious nibbles provided by her wealthy clients, Mrs Oakes' mince pies and the professor's sherry, like the high-minded academic conversation, were not to Belle's taste at all.

She *did* notice, though, how one of the professor's other students, a quiet, demure young woman with unexpectedly critically cool blue eyes, reacted in a way that was a good ten degrees *less* frosty when it was *Luc* who was addressing her and not Belle herself.

Not that Belle felt remotely threatened by or jealous of Harriet's obvious attraction to her husband. Why should she? Luc loved *her*, and would love her even more when they were cosily tucked up together in their lovely new bed with its wonderful headboard, she promised herself, and she happily contemplated writing a cheque to pay for it.

It had taken bribery and cajolery on a heroic scale to get her boss to agree that she could skip the firm's Christmas Eve get-together so that she could be at home with Luc when the bed was delivered. She had hardly seen anything of him over the previous month, or so it seemed, and she was looking forward to spending her few precious days off with him.

They were going to his parents for dinner on Christmas Day, and hers on Boxing Day, but they would have at least one night together in their new bed.

When she woke up on Christmas Eve morning Belle was so excited that she couldn't eat her breakfast. The house they had bought, their home, was everything that she wanted. It had the potential to make a wonderful home, and there was even the prospect of converting the loft above the garage into a self-contained bedsit, should the day arrive when they needed the services of a nanny.

Certainly, they both wanted children, but they had agreed that they were too young for them as yet. Luc wanted to wait until he had finished his studies, and from the tone of his conversation Belle had guessed that he would want her to give up her own job once they did have a family. She was not so sure that was something she would want to do, but there was plenty of time for her to talk Luc round to her point of view.

It was a pity that the bed had been so expensive, otherwise she might have been able to treat them to a visit to the January sales…

They desperately needed a decent sofa, and Belle rather liked the idea of them having two instead of the traditional one and a couple of armchairs. The cottage had a good-sized sitting room-cum-family room, as well as its large kitchen-cum-dining room, and on the other side of the entrance hall there was, much to her delight, a very respectably sized and pretty drawing room which ran the full length of the house. Plenty of scope for her home-making talents there. And the fact that the previous owners had been elderly meant that none of the attractive original features had been removed.

'You're looking very pleased with yourself,' Luc commented as he bent to kiss the top of her head and reach past her for the coffee pot.

'Mmm...' she agreed lazily, arching her neck and inviting him without a word to nuzzle the soft warm skin there.

'What have you got me for Christmas? I hope it's something very special,' she teased him, knowing full well that the only thing she really wanted from him, the gift she valued above everything else, was the one she already had: the gift of his love for her, his commitment to her.

'Well, I might just...' he began, and then stopped theatrically, his eyes sparkling with love and happiness as he teased her back. 'No guessing, though. You're just going to have to wait until tomorrow.'

'Tomorrow.' Belle pouted. 'But I thought we'd... I'm going to give you *my* present *today*. Tomorrow we're going to your parents...'

'Not until lunchtime,' Luc reminded her.

'It's going to be a very busy time,' Belle sighed. 'First dinner with your family, and then we're going to my parents on Boxing Day.'

The two families, who had not known one another before Luc and Belle had met, had become firm friends, and they lived close enough to make visiting one another quite easy, often sharing their homes with each other's families at special times like Christmas. On Christmas Day night Belle's parents, her elder sister and her husband and their two young children were joining Luc's parents and other members of his family. As a country vicar, Luc's father lived in a vicarage more than large enough to house everyone overnight, even if his small stipend meant that he could never afford to comfortably heat the vast Victorian church property.

Belle liked Luc's family, even if she sometimes found them a trifle unworldly compared with the people she mixed with in her working life. Certainly their values and beliefs were very much in tune with those of her own parents, and she particularly liked Luc's uncle and his wife, and their thirteen-year-old son who shared so much of a family resemblance with Luc that Belle had not been surprised when Luc's mother had told her that Andy looked just the same as Luc had done at his age.

Luc's father had studied theology at Cambridge, and there was a tradition in the family of its male members being Cambridge men.

Because they were spending so much time away from home over Christmas, Luc and Belle had agreed that it would be a waste to have a real Christmas tree, and one of Belle's clients had presented her with an artistic and very expensive Christmas arrangement from one of London's top florists, made up of bare twigs and glass baubles, which had caused Luc to raise his eyebrows a little.

'Don't you like it?' Belle had asked him.

'It's…it's very artistic,' Luc had replied cautiously, and then had added a rueful admission, 'At home we always have a huge tree loaded with masses of stuff. Not very arty, I suppose, but it always seems…right. Vicars' wives always have to recycle everything, and Ma used to encourage me to make my own decorations when I was small… Not very aesthetic, I know, but for me the real spirit of Christmas is the thought behind the gift, not its material value.'

He was right, of course, and Belle knew it, shared his sentiments, but somehow he had made her feel that her values were glossy and worthless and even, in some belittling way, that *she* was glossy and worthless too.

Today, though, was Christmas Eve, and very soon their own special Christmas present was going to arrive. And every Christmas from now on, when they woke up in their special bed, when they made love in it, they would remember this, their first Christmas in their new home. Belle couldn't wait to see the bed with its special headboard in situ, to polish and admire it.

It was almost lunchtime when the van finally arrived in the narrow country lane outside their house.

'What's this?' Luc frowned as the driver got out. 'They must be looking for somewhere else. We haven't ordered anything…'

'Yes, we have,' Belle corrected him excitedly, craning her neck so that she could see out of the window as the men went to the rear of the van. 'Well, *I* have. It's our Christmas present…well, mine to you…to us…to the house. It's the bed, Luc, the one I told you about…with the wonderful headboard,' she hurried on.

'The one we agreed we wouldn't have because it was too expensive?' Luc asked her quietly.

But Belle was oblivious to the cold undertone to his voice, too busy watching what was going on outside the window to be aware of the hurt look in his eyes as she agreed flippantly, 'That's the one.'

'You went ahead and bought it without telling me, despite what we'd agreed…'

Now Belle did look at him, alerted to his feelings by the ominous tone of his voice.

'I thought you'd be pleased,' she told him. 'It's a present...a surprise. Luc...what is it? Where are you going?' she demanded frantically as he turned his back on her and started to walk towards the back door.

'Luc, come back,' she pleaded, but it was too late, and she couldn't run after him because the delivery men were already coming up the path with their new bed.

Luc would come round when he saw how wonderful their bedroom looked with the bed and its headboard proudly adorning it, Belle decided two hours later, when the men had gone and she was standing in the doorway of their bedroom admiring her new acquisition. They would need to get some different bedding now, she acknowledged, frowning a little as she studied the pretty floral set they had been given as a wedding present. Somehow it just didn't do the new bed justice.

Luc had sanded and polished the old floorboards shortly after they had moved in, and they certainly set the bed off perfectly. It was, she knew, the kind of bed that demanded heavy Irish linen sheets scented with lavender, old-fashioned bed linen, all the traditional touches.

Luc would love that, waking up smelling of lavender… Luc…where was he? He had been gone a long time. She hoped he'd…

It was almost half an hour later when another van pulled up outside the house, a much shabbier, older one than the one which had delivered their new bed and its accoutrements, and, to her astonishment, she saw Luc climbing out of the driver's door.

'Luc.' She went to the front door and opened it, calling out anxiously to him. 'Where have you been?'

'To get your Christmas present,' he told her grimly.

Her Christmas present. In that old van… What on earth…? Warily she walked to the front gate and opened it, staring into the back of the van as Luc unlocked and raised the shutter door.

'What is it? What have you got in there?' she asked him uncertainly.

'I've already told you. Your Christmas present.'

As the last of the fading daylight filled the van and she saw inside it Belle's heart gave a shocked bound. There, in pieces, inside the van, was an old-fashioned bedframe, an obviously newly bought mattress and, tucked along one side of it, covered in a piece of old sheeting was the unmistakable shape of a wooden headboard.

'Luc…what have you done—' she began, and then stopped as he turned round and she saw his face.

She had never seen him look so bleak…so distant…so alien from her and to her.

'Very much the same as you've done. I've bought us a Christmas present. A new bed. For us…for you…' he told her in a voice that was icily polite and icily distant.

'That isn't new…the frame's old…' Belle began defensively. 'It looks…'

'It looks what?' Luc challenged her. 'It looks as though your colleagues…and your clients… would laugh at it, turn their materialistic designer noses up at it. Well, for your information, this bed belonged to my grandparents. They slept in it…cherished it…cared for it and valued it, just as my parents have done.'

'It's… It's…' Belle just didn't know what to say, and then, as Luc climbed into the van, the sheeting slipped off the headboard and the colour left her face completely. Unlike the frame itself, the headboard was quite plainly new. She could tell that because of the pretty carving on it, entwining their initials and the date of their marriage.

'Luc… You bought…' she began, but Luc was already shaking his head.

'I bought *nothing* apart from the mattress,' he told her grimly. 'The wood, good solid English oak, belonged to the father of one of my pupils. He gave it to me in exchange for his son's tuition. I did the carving myself. It isn't as fancy nor, I dare say, as desirable as the one you've bought, but…'

'You carved it…' Belle stopped him. '*You* carved it…'

'Yes.' Luc told her curtly, pushing the cloth back over it. 'But of course I realise that it won't come anywhere near to matching the one you've *bought*. The one *I* couldn't afford to buy you. It doesn't matter what I do or what I say, what I give you…how much I love you. The fact remains that you're the one who's supporting us both, financing us both…'

'Luc, what does *that* matter?' Belle protested. 'And besides, that's only temporary. When you get your fellowship…

'Oh, Luc, I love you so very much, and I love the headboard as well,' Belle told him tenderly—and she meant it.

\* \* \*

Luc's gift to her, his bed, was installed in their bedroom whilst the one she had bought was relegated to one of the guest bedrooms. They made up their quarrel, and the ones that followed it, but with each one the fabric of their marriage grew a little thinner, until eventually the day came when neither of them could be bothered to repair the worn patches any longer.

The crux came one weekend, when Belle arrived home early from an overseas conference to find that Luc, who had attended a dinner party in Cambridge the night before, had stayed over in Harriet Parish's rooms.

Luc protested in vain that it was all completely innocent, that he had simply had too much to drink to want to risk driving, that he loved her and that Harriet was simply a fellow student…a friend…

In the row that followed they said so many ugly and hurtful things to one another that Belle knew there was no going back. Not this time…

'You're so damn materialistic, you wouldn't know real value if it hit you on the head,' Luc accused her at one point during their argument. 'Money, money—that's all that matters to you.'

'Perhaps it would matter more to you if you were the one who earned it,' Belle retaliated. 'It's all very well for you, sitting up there above the rest of us in your ivory tower, Luc, but you seem to forget that without my earnings there would be no ivory tower for you to live in…'

And so it went on, the pair of them tearing at the precious fabric of their vulnerable marriage, rending it, ripping it, destroying it, in a frenzy of bitterness and petty resentments.

Belle moved out of the house that weekend and she never moved back.

Six weeks later she filed for divorce, refusing to even discuss with Luc any possibility of them getting back together. Ironically, the only thing she took from their marital home was the bed and headboard—not the one she had bought, that she had left behind, and for all she knew it was still there in the house with Luc, who had bought out her share of their marital home.

No, the headboard, the one that still graced the head of the bed in her small London home, was the one that Luc had made for her. Not that she had intended that to happen. The men she had sent to collect the other headboard and bed from the spare room had made a mistake, and somehow or other she had never bothered to correct it.

# CHAPTER TWO

'I MUST admit that Mum was stunned when you said that Luc had come round to deliver the invitation to you himself,' Joy, the happy bride, was saying now. 'I mean, we realised soon enough about the mistake. What on earth did he say? You must have been so surprised to open the door to see him there…'

'Mmm…'

'Luc, I was just saying to Belle that she must have been really surprised to open her front door and find you there,' Joy repeated breezily as her new husband's cousin suddenly materialised at Belle's side, apparently oblivious to the interest the fact that the two of them were standing amicably together was causing amongst their fellow wedding guests.

Luc's dark river-green eyes met Belle's honey-gold ones, exchanging a silent message.

'What on earth did you say to her? I mean, you hadn't spoken to one another for years…'

'Joy…' Andy cautioned his new bride, explaining to Belle and Luc, 'I think it must be the champagne on top of an empty stomach. She told me when we walked back down the aisle that she'd had three glasses whilst she was getting ready this morning…'

'No, four…' Joy corrected him, and then giggled.

'Darling, the photographer wants you,' her mother announced, coming up to the newly married pair and urging them to follow her.

'Oh, no more photographs,' Joy was complaining as her mother led her away.

'Saved by the flashbulb,' Luc commented humorously to Belle after they had gone.

'Mmm… You could hardly have told her what really happened, could you?'

'What? That you took one look at me, went white and practically fainted into my arms,' Luc commented.

'I'd been in bed with flu. I hadn't eaten anything for three days…' Belle defended herself. 'Besides,' she added slyly, 'I don't think *you'd* have wanted *me* telling Andy that you carried me upstairs to bed and started to undress me…'

'I did no such thing…'

'Yes, you did. My robe—'

'Your robe came off when I trod on the belt you had left undone as I picked you up. And I had to take you upstairs. All you have downstairs is your garage and an entry hall… And besides, if you will go completely naked under your robe… It was a freezing cold February day. I just wanted to get you somewhere warm. You frightened me to death, passing out like that. Mind you, I wasn't surprised. You were far too thin and frail…'

'I told you, I'd been ill. Which is why—'

'Goodness me, you two look very cosy. How long have you been married now? It must be over ten years, and still no children! Well, they say, don't they, that if you've none to make you laugh then you've none to make you cry?'

Great-Aunt Alice…

Belle gave Luc a speaking look above the elderly lady's head. There was no point in trying to explain her error, especially not when….

'Aunt Alice…there you are…' Carol, Belle's sister and the mother of the bride, came hurrying back, looking harassed as she put her arm around their elderly relative.

'Darling, I'm so sorry about all of this. You'll never guess what she's done now,' she hissed in a whisper to Belle, but before she could elucidate, David, her husband, was hurrying up to her telling her that the caterers wanted to speak urgently to her.

'Shame,' Luc commented, giving Belle a small smile as he watched his ex-sister-in-law's departing back. 'Now we'll never know just what it is that Great-Aunt Alice has done...'

'You mean what *else* she's done,' Belle corrected him drolly, returning his smile with a look in her eyes that caused a passing waitress, who was not aware of their divorced status, to reflect rather ruefully on the enviable ability of some couples to keep a passionate intensity in their relationship which was now only an increasingly blurred memory in her own. Mind you, she had to acknowledge fairly, it would be a very odd woman indeed who did *not* feel a twinge of sensual female excitement at the sight of a man as attractive as Luc. Her own husband, kind man though he was, was not exactly charismatic.

'Mmm... I must say I was rather taken aback when I received the wedding invitation addressed to both of us.'

'It *was* very thoughtful of you to take the trouble to deliver it by hand,' Belle responded mock demurely, her honey-gold eyes dancing with laughter—and something else, something deeper

and warmer that made Luc's breath catch slightly
in his throat. Belle had always had that special
something about her, a warmth and energy, a
vibrancy. He had noticed it about her the very first
time they had met.

'I was in London anyway,' Luc reminded her,
attempting to make light of the incident, but, like
hers, his eyes glowed hot with remembered
emotion, giving him away.

'It's rather warm in here. What do you say to us
taking the opportunity to get a little fresh air before
we go in for the wedding breakfast?' Luc suggested.

'People will talk,' Belle pointed out to him.
'They'll wonder what's going on…'

'Mmm…' Luc agreed, placing his hand on the
back of her waist and gently guiding her towards
the exit to the hotel's gardens.

'I'm glad to see that you've put some weight
back on.'

'I'd been ill,' Belle reminded him.

'You were skin and bone,' Luc continued. 'I
thought…'

'That I'd been pining away for you over the
years?'

Luc gave her a direct look.

'No. I didn't think that, Belle. I've got my

faults, I know that, but suffering from delusions has never been one of them.'

'Who says it would have been a delusion?' Belle surprised them both by admitting a little gruffly. 'There was a time when we first parted…' She paused, and then, her face clouding, told him, 'Oh, Luc…I was so dreadfully unhappy then, and—'

She stopped abruptly. It wasn't like her to admit to any kind of vulnerability, and she could see that Luc was as surprised by her admission as she herself was.

'If we weren't here…' he began, and Belle shook her head chidingly. But that didn't stop a tiny thrill of excitement running dangerously down her spine.

It *had* been a shock to open her front door that day and discover that her unwanted visitor was no less than Luc, her ex-husband, to whom she had neither spoken nor seen since their divorce seven years before.

The sight of him standing there, so tall and darkly handsome, so excessively and alluringly male and mature, had been more than her already overloaded weakened defence system had needed to send it into complete chaos.

As she'd clung to the front door she'd been

able to literally feel the blood draining down through her body at the same time as a weakening rush of dizzying faintness poured swiftly through it.

She had known what was going to happen, *known* she was going to faint, but at the same time she had known too that she simply did not have the strength or the will-power to halt it. Her last thought as Luc had masterfully reached out to catch her up in his arms had been how good he smelled, how good he *felt*…how good it was to be held so protectively and so safely in his arms.

Her faint had only lasted a couple of minutes, but that had been long enough for Luc to close her front door and carry her upstairs, through the living room of her small mews house and into her bedroom.

She had come round to discover that she was lying on her bed completely naked, with Luc leaning anxiously over her calling her name.

Even now, more than three months later, she still couldn't quite account for the effect, the erotic charge, the sheer inconsistency of the emotions which had allowed her to experience a previously unknown rush of intense female sensuality at the knowledge that she was naked whilst Luc was fully dressed. It was so out of character for her, so alien to what she might have expected to feel, that for several seconds it had robbed her of the ability to make any kind of response to Luc's presence other than to simply lie there watching him with widened golden eyes.

Later he had told her that it had been that look of dazed wonderment in place of the angry rejection and bitterness he had expected that had encouraged him to put aside his own protective defences and show her his concern and anxiety.

'Luc...' had been all she had been able to say, in an unfamiliarly weak and hesitant voice.

'You fainted,' he told her gently, his fingers stroking her forehead in reassurance.

'I know... I haven't been well,' she responded. 'I've had some kind of flu bug...'

'Which you no doubt refused to acknowledge and fought off until it *really* made you ill,' Luc countered a little grimly.

For a moment Belle was tempted to deny what he was saying, but the strong core of self-honesty she had developed since the failure of their marriage refused to let her.

'I had an important client meeting to attend,' she admitted. 'I should really have put it off, but this is such a cut-throat business I felt I couldn't afford to do so...'

Five years ago Belle had left the firm she had originally worked for and had set up in business on her own. Financially the rewards were not perhaps quite so high as they had been, and certainly the demands on her time and her energies were far greater, but so was the sense of satisfaction she gained from being her own boss.

Just recently, though, she found that she was deliberately ignoring opportunities to further her business and add to her client base, that she was beginning to respond to a previously unacknowledged need to allow things into her life other than her work, beginning to admit to a sense of awareness that there were certain things she was missing out on, certain emotional needs in her life which were not being met. But of course these were admissions she could not make to Luc, not when all those years ago Luc had accused her of putting her career above their marriage, when Luc had warned her that one day she would find herself lonely and alone.

'You always did make far too many demands on yourself,' Luc told her wryly, his criticism turning to concern as she suddenly started to shiver. 'You're freezing,' he told her almost accusingly.

This caused her to flash back at him, her eyes

brilliant with a mixture of fever and pride, 'And whose fault is that? I'm not the one who took off my robe.'

Immediately she wished she hadn't spoken, because now Luc, who before had only been looking at her face, watching her eyes, suddenly switched his gaze to her body.

Instinctively Belle tensed her muscles.

She had been a girl when she and Luc had first met. Now she was a woman. As a girl she had taken for granted the lush femininity of her body, the luminous sheen to her skin, the softness of her female flesh. Now she was older, her body shape different.

She could see the way Luc was frowning at her. No doubt she didn't compare well to whoever was currently sharing his bed. After all, a man in his position, a man with all his sexual assets, his charisma, his good looks, not to mention his powerful position as a leader in his scholastic field, was bound to be able to have his pick of all the best of his female students.

She, on the other hand… But, no, she wasn't going to start thinking about how empty her life was, how empty it had been since their divorce… Why should she? That had been her choice. There had been men, offers, opportunities; she had simply been too picky to accept any of them.

Luc was still frowning.

'You're too thin,' he told her abruptly. 'Are you eating properly?'

'It's fashionable to be thin,' Belle returned sharply, even though she knew perfectly well that her body weight was normally a good half-stone heavier than it was right now, and that she personally had thought herself a little on the thin side before this bout of flu had brought her weight down even further.

'Fashionable!' Luc's eyebrows rose.

'Yes,' Belle persisted. 'Just because *you* don't find my body attractive, that doesn't—'

'I didn't say I didn't find you attractive. I simply said you were too thin,' Luc interrupted softly. 'As a matter of fact—'

Quite what might have happened if he hadn't abruptly stopped speaking she didn't know, but he continued, his voice oddly hoarse, 'You need something to eat. Get into bed and don't you dare move so much as a muscle whilst I go downstairs and get you something.'

But she could hazard a very strong guess, Belle reflected with self-honesty after the door had closed after him. After all, whatever might have been the cause of their final quarrel, and her pride-fuelled abandonment of their marriage, it had had nothing to do with her not finding him physically attractive, or with her not wanting him…as a man…

Her face hot, she reminded herself that she was a woman in her mid-thirties, a woman whose body, whose emotions, whose most private physical needs had never once betrayed her in all the time she had been on her own.

It must be her weakened state that was making her so vulnerable, she reassured herself. Yes, that was it. That and the shock of seeing Luc so unexpectedly, of finding herself in such an unexpectedly dangerously intimate situation with him.

Thinking of which, where on earth *was* her robe?

She had just reached the bedroom door when Luc opened it from the other side, frowning severely at her when he saw that she had disobeyed his edict.

'You shouldn't be out of bed. You've already passed out once,' he reminded her severely.

'I was looking for my robe,' Belle informed him, trying to summon what dignity she could. No small task when one was standing shivering and nude in front of the man who had every reason to find the sight of one's naked form less than physically appealing.

'Get into bed. I'll go and find it for you,' Luc told her with unexpected gentleness. 'At least you've got the sense to keep this place properly heated, even if you *don't* seem able to feed yourself. What on earth do you live on, Belle? There is hardly anything in your fridge or cupboards.'

'That's because I prefer to buy fresh food,' Belle returned quickly and loftily. 'And I've been too ill to feel like going out shopping for the last few days.'

'Mmm… Well, I've managed to find a can of soup and some eggs. Drink your soup whilst I go back down and make you an omelette.'

He was certainly behaving very masterfully, Belle acknowledged as she tucked hungrily into her soup when he had gone back to the kitchen.

But hadn't that always been one of the causes of their problems? The fact that it had irked his male pride that *she* had been the main provider. Not that he had tried to dominate her. No. She could never have loved him the way she had had he been like that. But she had always felt that he had subtly punished her for not being more helpless, more financially dependent upon him.

The warmth of her bed now that she had snuggled under the duvet and the blissful comfort of the hot soup in her stomach combined to make her feel relaxed and sleepy. So much so that by the time Luc returned with the promised omelette she was already half asleep. The sight of the amount of food he had piled onto the plate brought her sharply awake, though. Indignantly she stared at it.

'I can't eat all that,' she protested. 'It's indecent. There must be at least a dozen eggs there…'

'Not quite,' Luc told her cheerfully, without any apparent remorse. 'Actually we're *both* going to eat it. I don't care to miss out on my meals even if you do,' he told her severely. 'And since I could only find one plate, we shall have to share.'

'The others are in the dishwasher,' Belle informed him, and then added defensively, 'I'm a single woman living alone, Luc. I don't have either the space or the need to own a full twelve-place dinner service.'

'Surely you entertain sometimes?'

'Not really. I prefer to take business clients out, it's much easier and more professional. And besides—' she chewed a little betrayingly on her bottom lip '—it isn't always a good idea to invite male clients into one's home…'

'You've had problems with men…clients…

behaving badly towards you?' Luc demanded fiercely.

'Er…it was a long time ago, when we first divorced and it was probably my own fault. I didn't realise the false message I could be giving inviting a client home.'

'He frightened you? Hurt you? Who…?'

'Nothing like that,' Belle hastened to assure him. 'It was just that there was a rather…embarrassing episode. A misunderstanding, really, that was all.'

'You mean one of your clients tried to…?'

'I've told you, Luc, it was all a long time ago, and fortunately he accepted that there'd been a misunderstanding. But after that I made the decision not to invite clients home—not that the way I run my life, either private or professional, is any business of yours.'

'Don't you ever find it lonely living alone?' he asked her, completely throwing her. But before she could make the defensively protective denial that was hovering on her lips he further confounded her by admitting quietly, 'I know that I do…'

'You…you live alone…?' Belle raised her eyes to his face.

'I've lived alone since you left,' he told her simply.

Belle's appetite had completely deserted her, and oddly Luc didn't seem to be particularly hungry either.

'Belle…'

'Luc…'

'I'm glad to see you kept the bedhead,' he told her huskily, and then he lifted his hand and reached past her to trace the initials and the date he had carved into it. 'I have to admit it isn't anywhere near so handsome, though, as the one you bought.'

'Nor so expensive,' Belle said quietly, dropping her gaze from his so that he wouldn't guess that the cost she *was* referring to was not in terms of the money she had spent on the bedhead, but the reckless wastage, the dreadful continuing payment with increasingly heavy interest she was still having to make in terms of broken dreams and lost love.

'Belle…'

As he withdrew his hand from the bedhead and straightened up, Belle lifted her head.

His gaze met hers and held it. Her whole body started to tremble, her heart beating far too fast.

Luc started to lower his head towards hers. He was going to kiss her. Belle just knew it. Her heart was racing so fast that she thought it might explode. Automatically she closed her eyes. She could almost feel the warmth of Luc's mouth against her own, taste the wonderful familiarity of his kiss, breathe in his special scent, feel…

'I must go…'

Abruptly her eyes snapped open. Luc *wasn't* going to kiss her after all.

'It was very thoughtful of you to call,' she told him stiffly. 'I'll get in touch with Carol and tell her about Great-Aunt Alice's mistake.'

'It's quite a coincidence that your niece and my cousin should be marrying…'

'Yes…I suppose it is.'

'Andy was telling me the last time I saw him that he's applied to finish his training in the same town where Joy has just been appointed a junior registrar at the local hospital.'

Immediately Belle guessed what he must be thinking.

'And of course you don't approve of that. No doubt you think she should be the one to follow *him*?'

'On the contrary,' Luc replied evenly. 'I think that he's a very fortunate young man to have a woman who loves him so much that she's prepared to take on the burden of being the major wage-earner until he's fully qualified. After all, if Andy hadn't changed his mind about the career path he wanted to follow, he would be qualified himself by now.

'I still think it's ironic that it takes longer to train to be a vet than a doctor, but I hope that Andy will appreciate both Joy and her love, and that he doesn't allow his male pride—'

He broke off and looked away from her. 'Fortunately his generation has a far healthier and more flexible attitude towards interchanging the traditional roles than ours perhaps did.'

Belle tried to speak, but found that she couldn't articulate a single word because of the lump in her throat.

This was the first time Luc had ever acknowledged that he could have been wrong. She *knew* that *she* had made mistakes, gone about things the wrong way, been rather less careful of his male pride than she might have been, but this was the first time she had felt that Luc, too, might have regrets, doubts about the things he had done, the way he had behaved…reacted. Perhaps if she had known that then…if they had sat down together like this then and talked… But Luc wasn't sitting down now; he was getting up. He was going away—leaving her—his Good Samaritan duties done.

Belle watched as he walked towards the door.

'Thank you for…for the soup,' she told him gruffly as he opened it, and then she looked away, closing her eyes, unable to bear watching him go out of her life…again…

When several seconds went by and she hadn't heard the final click of the door she opened her eyes again, widening them as she saw how close Luc was to the bed. How close he was to her.

'You don't have to thank me Belle—not ever—not for *anything*,' he told her, and then he did what he hadn't done before. He bent his head and kissed her.

A brief, non-sexual, amicable little kiss—or so he'd said it was supposed to be, when he'd told her later—but somehow their lips, their mouths, their senses had other ideas, and the brief brush of his cool mouth against hers became something warmer, deeper… longer…and far, far more intimate as their mouths clung together.

'I shouldn't be doing this. You're not well,' Luc groaned, but he still took her in his arms, holding her tightly against his heart so that she could feel its fierce thud as he cupped her face in his hands and looked deeply into her eyes.

Very tenderly Luc caressed her lips with his.

Somewhere in the distance Belle could hear a noise, shrill, intrusive, unwanted. Her telephone was ringing. Reluctantly she broke the kiss.

'It's Carol,' she told Luc as she recognised her sister's number on the visual display unit.

When she picked up the receiver she could hear her sister's voice announcing frantically, 'Belle, something dreadful's happened. Great-Aunt Alice has sent…'

Belle could see Luc walking towards the door. She wanted to call out to him to stay…not to go…not to leave her. But she was a grown woman, and grown women did not give in to such foolish urges, such foolish emotions.

Covering the receiver, she called out instead, 'I'm afraid I'm going to have to ask you to let yourself out…'

'Belle? Belle, is someone there with you?' she could hear Carol demanding curiously.

'It was just…an unexpected visitor…' Belle responded as casually as she could as Luc closed the bedroom door very gently behind himself.

And it was, after all, the truth.

Carol, at any rate, seemed perfectly happy with her explanation, continuing urgently, 'I don't know *how* to tell you this, but Great-Aunt Alice has only gone and sent your wedding invitation to Luc. Belle! Belle, are you still there?'

'I'm still here,' Belle confirmed.

Ten minutes later, after her sister had rung off, Belle warned herself sternly that there was no point in wondering or dwelling on what might have happened if her sister hadn't rung up, if Luc had continued to kiss her, if she had actually dared to give in to the emotions, the sensations that had been flooding her.

With Luc's lips caressing hers it had been extraordinarily easy to forget their quarrels and the harsh words they had said to one another in the final, agonising dying throes of their marriage and oh, so easy to remember instead the love they had once shared.

Had *once* shared?

Shakily Belle closed her eyes. It must be the weakening effect of her flu that was making her feel like this, making her remember…regret… wish… But the way she had felt just now, when Luc had kissed her, had been the reaction of the woman she was now to the man he was now, she acknowledged with painful honesty. She had wanted him as the man he was, had felt that age-old female response to his nearness and his touch as the woman she had grown into.

Not wanting to pursue such a dangerous train

of thought, Belle punched her pillow and told herself that she ought to be trying to sleep and get herself better.

Belle was asleep when Luc let himself back into her small house several hours later. He had found her spare keys hanging on a hook in the kitchen, neatly labelled. He had been reluctant to leave her on her own, having seen how ill she looked. She was far too thin, far too pale, and no doubt she was working far too hard and neglecting to look after herself properly.

A wry smile curled his mouth. One of her complaints about him had been that he fussed too much.

'When I'm hungry, I'll eat,' had been her standard response to him in the old days, when he had complained about their lack of ordered meal times.

These days he could sympathise more with that view. He certainly found no pleasure in going home to an empty house and cooking for himself, and as a consequence he found that he tended to snatch meals on the run between lectures and meetings. But at least he could dine in hall if he wanted to—the academic's version of the businessman's 'business lunches', he acknowledged ruefully as he climbed the stairs and went into

Belle's kitchen to unpack the groceries he had bought whilst he was out.

No doubt she would be furious with him for what she would undoubtedly consider to be his unwarranted interference. But, deny it though she would, there was still, on his part at least, a sense of there being a bond between them, a relationship, and he could no more have returned to Cambridge after his meeting with fellow academics without returning to check that she was all right than he could have walked away when she'd opened the door to him and he had seen how ill she looked.

It was true that all those years ago, after the initial shock, and his instinctive attempt to deny what was happening, he had been forced to acknowledge that, given the growing frequency and intensity of their quarrels, and the disharmony between them, he'd had no option but to accept Belle's decision that she wanted a divorce. Certainly it had seemed impossible at the time for them to be able to reconcile their growing differences, but in the years since then his position had given him plenty of opportunity to observe and consider the changes taking place in the way the sexes related to one another and ran their relationships.

It was no extraordinary thing at all now for a female student to take on the financial responsibility of helping to support her partner, or to go on to become the main breadwinner whilst he opted to continue his studies; why, even some of his female colleagues were openly outspoken about the fact that they, as highly qualified women earning good salaries, actively *preferred* to have a partner who was happy to take a more passive but nevertheless extremely important and supportive role in their relationship.

'It's just too exhausting battling to accommodate two major egos,' one female colleague had told him frankly, when they had been discussing the subject. 'Quite honestly, whilst there's a part of me that will always be drawn to the high-powered "Alpha"-type male biologically speaking, as a thinking woman, I *know* that I have a far better chance of happiness and a far pleasanter life with a man who is prepared to let me take the lead role.'

Not that he and Belle's relationship had been quite like that.

He personally had *always* considered Belle to be his equal in *every* way, although sexually she had tended to look to him to initiate their lovemaking, at least in the earlier stages of their relationship. If he was honest, Luc had to admit that his own inflexible old-fashioned male attitude to money had been the maggot which had eaten away at the foundations of their marriage. Although he had always been too proud to admit it to her, it *had* irked him, *hurt* him, that she had been the one to provide the major part of their income, and because of that he had been less than generous in sharing the pleasure it had given her to buy things for their home…and for him.

Yes, there had been faults on both sides, but…

But it was too late now to go back and rewrite the past. Not the past, maybe, but there was still the present…and the future. Luc paused in the act of closing the fridge door.

Holding Belle in his arms earlier, he had been overwhelmed by an impulse…a need…to take things further. Very thoughtfully he made his way to Belle's bedroom. She was asleep, lying curled up like a small child, looking very alone in the large bed. And she had let her guard down enough with him to imply she had not shared that bed with anyone else.

Which put them both on an equal footing.

Luc knew men who complained that the sexual frustration of being without a partner drove them to irrational excesses of behaviour and unsuitable relationships… But, desperately though he had missed Belle, and the intimacy of their lovemaking, he had never experienced any desire to fill her place with another woman, another body…any body…just to ease the sexual ache of her absence. And yet earlier today, holding her, he had been sharply and shockingly reminded of just how powerfully potent the male sex drive could be, of just how determinedly and dangerously it could overrule reason and logic.

If the intensity with which he had once wanted Belle, and loved her, had dimmed over the years, then being so close to her had certainly given him a sharp reminder of just how it had once been.

Luc sat down on the bed beside her, watching her, remembering.

The first time he had held her, really properly held her, she had literally trembled with excitement in his arms. When he had kissed her he had felt as though he had instantly become Master of the Universe, Lord of Eternity, no mere mortal any longer, at once so strong and powerful that there was nothing, no goal beyond his reach, and at the same time so achingly vulnerable that she could have reduced him to emotional dust simply by refusing him her smile.

It had been the love of poets and sages, beyond

reason, beyond logic, and certainly beyond the control of a mere mathematician, and miraculously she had felt the same.

It was, they had both sworn, a love that would last for ever; they were soulmates, two perfect halves of an even more perfect whole. So why and how had they managed to destroy it? Not so much, perhaps, through human frailty, but rather through human strength, pride, arrogance, mistaken belief on the part of both of them that they were wholly in the right.

It was no doubt fitting that he should be examining the flaws which had led to the destruction of their marriage now—if not on the eve of his cousin's marriage to Belle's niece then certainly on the runway approach to it. Not that Andy was likely to ask him for his advice, or his admission on where he had gone wrong.

He was still deep in thought when Belle opened her eyes. At first she thought she was seeing a mirage. She had seen Luc leave with her own eyes, but here he was, sitting on the side of her bed as he looked towards the window, his expression, in repose, both stern and sad.

Instinctively she reached out to touch him.

Instantly he turned towards her.

'Belle, you're awake. How are you feeling?'

'Better,' she told him, dismissing the subject of her health in favour of something which interested her far more.

'What are you doing here? I thought you'd gone.'

'I had…I had a meeting to attend, otherwise… I was concerned about you. You shouldn't neglect your health, you know. You're…'

'Not getting any younger. I know,' Belle agreed dryly.

'I've bought you some groceries,' Luc informed her. 'If you're hungry.'

I'm not… Belle had been about to say, but instead—as she would be the first to admit to herself later—a little deviously she fibbed.

'Well, yes, I am a little, but I really don't feel like getting up and cooking. My head still aches and…'

'You stay right where you are,' Luc commanded her, getting up. 'I'll do the cooking.'

'Are you sure? Don't you have to get back?'

'Yes and no,' Luc told her promptly, holding her eyes as he added quietly, 'After all, what is there for me to go back to other than an empty house?

'I'll go and make us both something to eat, and then, if you feel up to it, Belle, I'd like us to talk.'

'Talk?' Steadily Belle returned his gaze, her

own never faltering as she read the message he was giving her with his eyes. 'I feel up to it,' she responded huskily.

# CHAPTER THREE

'BELLE, Carol says it's time for the wedding break-fast. Carol's got the reception line organised to go in. It's a shame that you won't be on the top table, but…'

'Mum, I really don't mind,' Belle reassured her mother. 'After all, I'm only Joy's aunt, not her mother or her bridesmaid…'

'I can't believe the last wedding we had in the family was yours and Luc's. I saw him earlier. He made a point of coming over to talk to your father and me…'

Belle smiled and waited patiently, knowing what was coming next. Her mother had never made any secret of the fact of how much she had liked Luc.

'I hate to say it, Belle,' she had told her younger daughter unhappily after the divorce, 'but this is what happens when a woman puts her job before her husband.'

'Mum...*I'm* the one who wanted the divorce, not Luc,' Belle had reminded her mother sharply. 'And as for putting my job first—'

She had stopped, knowing that there was no point in arguing with her mother and upsetting her. She was a woman of her time and had what Belle considered to be antiquated, old-fashioned views about a woman's role in life. She had worked as a secretary until Carol had been conceived, and after that she had stayed at home to look after her daughters and her husband. Not out of any sense of duty, but because that was what she had wanted to do.

'Carol's put you on a table with—'

'Great-Aunt Alice. I know,' Belle acknowledged, dutifully smiling at her father as he came over to join them.

Joy had opted for informal round tables for seating her wedding guests. Belle's was in the middle of the room, commanding an excellent view of the other guests, but as she approached it her eyebrows lifted slightly in amused surprise as she saw Luc standing beside the chair next to her own—the chair which should have been occupied by Belle's Great-Aunt Alice.

As she joined him, Belle cast a discreet look at the place-cards. They read 'Mrs Isabelle Crawford' and 'Mr Lucius Crawford.'

'Another demonstration of Aunt Alice's handiwork,' Belle murmured to Luc as the other guests sharing their table reacted to their joint presence with varying degrees of astonishment and confusion.

'Well, let's just say that she was certainly the inspiration for it,' Luc responded in an amused undertone.

Her eyes brimming with laughter, Belle looked at Luc. 'Where *is* Aunt Alice, by the way?' she asked him.

'Er...I *was* to have been seated with my godfather....'

'Admiral Rogers?'

'Mmm...'

'Well, I hope you aren't going to regret your moment of Machiavellian interference with Joy's table plan,' Belle warned him, 'because I'm certainly going to. People are going to think it very odd to see us seated together in apparent amity...'

'Mmm... But after all, it isn't as though this is the first time lately that we've shared a meal on... amicable terms...is it?' Luc reminded her.

'No,' Belle agreed, shaking her head at him as a secret amused smile passed between them.

* * *

It had been late in the evening when Luc had eventually left. They'd talked, but by mutual agreement they'd avoided going too deep into painful areas on this occasion. He'd cooked them both a meal, and then insisted that the two glasses of red wine he had coaxed Belle to drink would be good for her and help build her up.

'Red wine *is* good for you,' he had insisted when she had raised her eyebrows.

'And chocolates,' she had semi-mocked him as she'd popped one of the delicious hand-made truffles that were her favourites into her mouth.

'The Aztecs considered chocolate to be an aphrodisiac,' he had continued blandly. 'And I've certainly no reason to argue with that.'

Belle remembered how she had blushed—and why. Long, long before the current fad for chocolate body paint there had been a certain occasion when, as a result of a cosy winter evening spent in front of an open fire, Luc had insisted on licking away the remnants of the melted chocolate she had dropped first from her fingers and then from the vee of flesh exposed by her robe where it had fallen open.

The sizzling sensuality she had experienced beneath the lazy, deliberate brush of his tongue against her skin had driven her to a frenzy of need which had resulted in her punishing him for his slow, lingering tantalisation of her body and her senses with an equally intimate exploration of his body with her own fingers and lips.

After that, the gift of chocolates between them had possessed a special intimacy and meaning, although she had assumed when he produced them this evening that he must have forgotten this.

Now, as he looked from her mouth to her fingertips, and then back to her mouth again, Belle knew that whilst he might not have bought the chocolates to remind her of that occasion—why, after all, should he have done so?—she *had* been reminded of it, *was* being reminded of it, and extremely forcibly, by a body and a set of emotions which, no matter how strictly she had fought to control them, had never truly forgiven her for denying them, and certainly had never, ever forgotten just how intense and magical the sexual rapport between her and Luc had been.

Every day for a week after that Luc rang her to see how she was feeling.

By the third day she was back at work, unofficially, at least, working from home, her body tensing every time the telephone rang in case it was Luc calling and then, abruptly, seven days after his initial visit the calls ceased.

Belle couldn't believe how bereft she felt, or how much she missed the sound of Luc's voice, as warm and rich as dark melting chocolate, touching her senses and unleashing emotions, longings, needs, she had thought long ago safely banished.

By the end of the second day without a call from him she was reduced to virtually willing him to ring, snapping unforgivably at both her mother and her sister for telephoning her and not being him.

'You need a holiday,' her mother chided her. 'You work far too hard, darling. Which reminds me. Your father and I were wondering if you could possibly manage to house-sit for us whilst we go away. Carol would do it, but with the wedding so close…'

'Don't worry, I'll do it,' Belle confirmed. She had been thinking for some time of relocating, moving herself and her business outside London. After all, her parents weren't getting any younger. Her sister and the rest of her family were all based in Cambridgeshire, her roots were there, and certainly with the aid of modern technology she could easily work from there. Besides which…

Belle wasn't sure when she had realised she was tired of opening her eyes in the morning and only being able to see a small patch of clear sky, or when she had first had that sharp yearning for the familiar flatness of the fens, the wideness of its skies. She just knew that her city life had somehow or other lost its appeal.

It was ironic to remember now how she had berated Luc, before they had found their pretty cottage, for refusing to transfer to the LSE so that they could both be based in London.

'I'm not a city person, Belle,' he had told her quietly, looking at her. 'I want our children to grow up in the same country environment that we both enjoyed.'

Their children... It had been on the tip of Belle's tongue to remind him just how impossible it was for her to even *think* of taking time out to have one child, never mind children... But instead she had demanded tartly, 'You're running ahead a little, aren't you, Luc? I can't afford to finance a nanny as well as your studies.'

It was a comment that she had bitterly regretted once she had made it. It had shamed both of them, and she had hated herself for the look she had seen in his eyes, but the thought that Luc was already planning ahead for their family, when she felt under so much pressure at work, when she had so little time and so many responsibilities, had panicked her into lashing out verbally at him.

Now things were different. Now career women of her age, all too conscious of the fast ticking of their biological clocks, were choosing the option of children without even a permanent partner, never mind the burdens on their careers, rather than miss out on the maternal boat. She envied them the single-mindedness that enabled them to make such a decision. Perhaps her own deep-rooted belief that a child thrived best surrounded by the love of both its parents sprang from the nurturing she had received in her own very happy childhood.

But that hadn't stopped her thinking some-times that if she and Luc had had a child—children—it might have compelled them both to work a little harder at protecting their marriage. Or, conversely, it might have led to her being a single parent, struggling to bring up a child and manage her career as well.

She had surprised herself two years before when she'd discovered how easy it was to make the decision to downsize her business life, to leave behind the hectic life she had lived for so long and set up in business on her own, on a much smaller scale, with only a handful of carefully picked clients—clients who shared her own view that with wealth came a certain moral responsibility not to abuse those who did not possess such assets.

She was proud of the way she was guiding her clients to combine sound investment and financial management with an awareness of the moral issues involved in making profits, an awareness of other people's poverty, and, increasingly now, prospective clients were approaching her because they had heard of her humanitarian beliefs and record.

Three days after Luc had last rung her, he finally telephoned.

'I don't know if you've received a copy of the wedding present list or not yet,' he began, 'but it occurred to me that if we were to club together we could potentially remove one of the larger items from the list.'

'We could, but—'

'Why don't we discuss it over dinner?' Luc interrupted her.

'I…' Belle opened her mouth to refuse, but discovered instead that her voice seemed to have deserted her.

'I've got to come down to London to see a colleague the day after tomorrow. If you're free that evening I could call for you…'

'I… Yes. Very well,' Belle agreed weakly.

* * *

Luc took her to San Lorenzo which, in itself, surprised her. Not so much because of its reputation as one of the best and most expensive restaurants in London—after all, as a Fellow he was now hardly the struggling young academic he had been when she had first met him—but because she hadn't really thought that such a high-profile society place would be to his taste. What surprised her even more, though, was the discovery that the staff knew him well enough to have remembered his name.

Sensing her surprise, Luc waited until the wine waiter had gone before explaining easily to her, 'One of my students used to insist on bringing me here for her tutorials.'

'Really?' Belle gave him an icy little smile. 'I though it was the tutor who dictated where a tutorial would take place, not the student.'

'Mmm…but this student was rather special.'

'Oh.' Belle's voice had grown even icier.

'Mmm…' Luc smiled reminiscently, apparently unaware of the frigid atmosphere Belle was generating. 'She was a second or third cousin to the owners of the restaurant, and she was working here to help finance her way through university as a mature student—'

'She was a *mature* student?' Belle interrupted him sharply.

'Well, yes…'

'How mature?' Belle demanded instantly.

'Oh…pretty mature… Around fifty or so…'

Immediately Belle started to relax, unaware of the look of wry comprehension mixed with tenderness that Luc was giving her. She had always been very passionate and, whilst not possessive, certainly inclined to be very protective of their relationship. He, on the other hand, as he openly had to admit, had been rather immaturely jealous. He re-angled his chair so that the darkly handsome young waiter who was currently studying her with burning admiration was blocked out of her view.

It was late when they finally left the restaurant, and it was Luc who commented wryly as he hailed a taxi, 'We still haven't decided about the wedding present.'

'No,' Belle agreed.

They had been too busy talking about themselves to discuss anything so mundane as the rival attractions of a washing machine or a dishwasher, the two items they had narrowed their choice down to.

'I must have made you so angry sometimes,' Belle had commented at one point during the

evening, when they had been discussing the break-
down of their marriage.

'Not angry, no,' Luc had countered quickly,
shaking his head and reaching across the table to
take hold of her hand in both of his.

'Hurt, rejected, and even at times demeaned,
yes. But angry, no! It hurt me that I couldn't afford
to provide you with the material things you
wanted, that *I* wasn't the one paying the mortgage,
that *I* couldn't go out and order that bed you
wanted…'

'You were a proud man, and I should have
realised how much what I was doing was hurting
you,' Belle had groaned remorsefully, but once
again Luc had shaken his head.

'No. If I was proud then it was a false pride. My
pride should have been in *you*, in what you were
doing for both of us, in what we were achieving
by working together.

'I made a lot of mistakes, Belle, but so far as I
am concerned the biggest mistake of all was the
one I made when I let you go.'

'I made mistakes as well,' was all Belle had
been able to whisper in response.

Now, on the way home in the taxi, she was
mentally examining what he had said. Uncertainly
she darted a glance at him. His face was turned

towards the window, so that she could only see his profile. To say he regretted their divorce was one thing; to say that he still loved her was something else again.

'Have you got time to come in for a cup of coffee?' Belle asked him uncertainly as the taxi drew up outside her home. 'We ought to make a decision about the present.'

'Yes, of course,' Luc agreed immediately.

The flowers he had given her when he'd picked her up were in water in the kitchen. As she waited for the coffee Belle breathed in their scent, touching the petals with gentle fingers.

Luc was standing in the sitting room removing his jacket as she walked in. He glanced at his watch and then cursed.

'What is it? What's wrong?' Belle asked him.

'I've just realised that it's half past twelve, and not half past eleven as I thought,' he told her. 'That means I've missed the last train. Never mind. I'll book myself into a hotel.'

'You can't do that,' Belle protested. 'Not at this time of night. I…you could stay here…the sofa converts into a bed and…' Uncertainly her voice trailed away. Staying here with her was probably the last thing Luc wanted to do.

But just as she was wishing that she had not

spoken so impetuously, she heard him saying warmly, 'Well, if you're sure you don't mind, I *would* be very grateful.'

'This reminds me of the first time you stayed over with me,' Luc told her five minutes later, when they were drinking their coffee.

'You mean the night you'd taken me to a college ball and your car wouldn't start so we had to spend the night together in your rooms?'

'Mmm…that's the one,' Luc agreed reminiscently.

As she looked hurriedly away from him Belle hoped he hadn't noticed the way she had to wrap her hands tightly around her coffee mug to stop her fingers from trembling.

That had been the first night they had actually been lovers. She had known how she felt about Luc then, of course, and she had been pretty sure that he shared her feelings, but that night had been the first night she had allowed herself to give way to those feelings.

She could still vividly remember how nervous she had felt when she had walked with Luc to his rooms. There had been no question of him deliberately contriving to have his car break down—they had discovered later that the part in question had been slowly wearing away for some time—but there had been something about the way he had held her earlier when they had been dancing, the way he had kissed her, the passion with which he had whispered to her that she was the most beautiful girl at the ball, the most beautiful girl in the whole world, that had warned her how potentially dangerous it would be for them to be alone together.

He hadn't touched her at first, explaining almost formally that since there was only one bed *he* would sleep on the floor, but then she had started to shiver, as much with nerves as cold, and he had come over to her, slipping off his dinner jacket to place it on her shoulders. The moment she had felt the warmth of his fingertips against her skin she had been lost.

The sexual tension between them even in the short time they had known one another had become increasingly hard to ignore each time they touched, kissed...*breathed*... It had been there, that night, and as her body shuddered helplessly and visibly at his touch, Belle had known that the moment had come to succumb to it.

As she'd turned towards him his jacket had slid disregarded to the floor. She'd raised her face towards him, her eyes misting with emotional tears as he'd reached out and cupped it with hands that

trembled just as much as her body had done. He had started to kiss her, softly, gently, and then, abruptly, he had stopped, withdrawing his mouth from hers.

Deprived of its warm, sensuous contact, Belle had opened her eyes to stare with uncertain questioning into his.

'I can't...' he'd begun hoarsely, and then stopped. 'I don't...'

He had closed his eyes and leaned away from her, the moonlight picking out the arch of his throat and the tensing of his jaw. His eyes had closed in some kind of male anguish. Opening his eyes, he'd looked directly at her and told her thickly, 'Belle, if I touch you now...kiss you now...it won't...I can't...it won't be gentle,' he had finally told her rawly. 'I want you too much to be able to...'

Instinctively Belle had known what he meant, what he was trying to tell her. Boldly she'd stepped towards him, and away from her virginal girlhood.

'Show me,' she'd commanded him softly. And then she had simply stood waiting, watching him.

She had known, felt the difference the moment he touched her. His fingers had burned against her skin, almost as hotly and excitingly as the look she'd seen in his eyes. But that had been nothing compared to the tension, the need, the hunger she'd felt in him when he had kissed her, his mouth almost bruising the softness of hers as he'd given way to the intensity of his passion before lifting his mouth to apologise disjointedly, touching her lips with his fingertips, telling her that he was thoughtless, selfish, that he had no right…

'Stop talking and kiss me again,' Belle had interrupted him huskily. This time she had returned his passion measure for measure, biting wantonly at his bottom lip, running her tongue-tip excitedly along the shape of his mouth, opening hers to the hot thrust of his tongue when he'd reacted to her sensuality. How long they had stood like that, kissing one another, *devouring* one another, *consuming* one another in the fierce passion of their mutual need, Belle had had no idea. She'd only known that when they finally broke apart it was with one accord, as though their every movement had been perfectly choreographed. As they'd undressed one another she'd had no sense of shyness or uncertainty; there had been no clumsiness or awkwardness, only the soft slithering sound of their clothes falling away from their bodies and then that fierce, primitive moment of mutual, visual examination, of studying one another as they'd stood clothed only in the soft shadows of Luc's room.

It had been seeing the way Luc had looked at her that had made her lift her head in pride and joyous recognition of the full power of her femininity, glorying in Luc's reaction to it and her own sense of pleasure and strength in the message his reaction had given her. She was beautiful, desirable, *loved*. She had seen all that and more in his eyes.

And she'd felt the same way about him. Very gently she'd reached out and touched him, carefully placing her lips to the hollow at the base of his throat, her hands spread out across the breadth of his chest.

Very delicately she had breathed in the scent of his skin, and then very deliberately she had tasted him.

Her touch had had the effect of smashing the barrier holding back an oceanic dam, but she had given herself willingly, gladly, voluptuously and joyously to the tumult, making herself a part of its power. Later, exhausted, beached, bleached dry, light-headed with the release and emotionally intoxicated with the euphoria of their love, they'd promised one another that this was just the beginning, the explosive starburst of a whole new universe of love that they would share for ever.

The following morning she had woken up in Luc's bed with Luc's dinner jacket draped over her naked body. On the empty pillow beside her had been a red rose, and attached to its stem had been an engagement ring…

She glanced instinctively now at her left hand, and realised to her chagrin that Luc had done the same.

'You're still wearing it,' he told her softly, not just echoing her thoughts but showing, too, that he had guessed just what she had been remembering.

'It's a little bit on the tight side, and I'd have had to have had it cut off,' she told him, not quite truthfully. But there was no way she was going to admit to him just *how* she still came to be wearing it, no way she was going to tell him about that night, less than a year after their divorce had become final, the night which had been the anniversary of the night he had given the ring to her when, overcome by sentiment and longing, she had slipped it back onto her finger and had left it there. No need, either, to mention just how often in times of anxiety and stress she touched it, twisting it, gaining comfort from its presence and from the memories she had learned to cherish.

'Besides, *you* still wear your wedding ring,' she pointed out, gesturing to the plain gold band on his left hand.

'*I* wasn't the one who wanted a divorce,' he told her sombrely.

'It's getting late,' Belle told him hurriedly. 'We ought to go to bed—' She stopped, and bent her head so that the thick cascade of her hair fell across her face, concealing its hot colour.

'I…I haven't anything I can offer you to wear, I'm afraid,' she apologised. 'I'll just go and get some clean towels and some bedlinen.

She kept the duvet for the sofa bed in the top of the wardrobe in her own bedroom. It was, after all, seldom used. She was standing on her dressing table stool trying to get it down when Luc saw what she was doing and came in to help her.

'Let me do that. You might fall,' he chided her.

'No, I won't,' Belle denied, and of course promptly did, bringing the duvet with her, so that as Luc rushed forward to catch her it unfurled, engulfing them both.

She was wearing a silk jersey black dress she had bought in Italy, very plain in design and very fluidly sexy. As she tumbled it rode up, revealing the soft flesh of her thigh and the wispily brief briefs she was wearing underneath.

Luc, who had put out his hand to steady her, discovered that instead of touching her waist his hand was actually resting on the smoothly naked flesh of her leg.

Were his fingertips actually stroking her skin, not just touching it? Belle wondered dizzily. Or was she just imagining it, *wanting* it…

'Belle.'

She heard him whisper her name, and instinctively she looked up at him.

'You haven't changed,' he told her softly. 'You still do things to me that…' He groaned rawly under his breath as he leaned over her. Belle felt her stomach muscles clench as she recognised that he was going to kiss her. But she didn't do anything to try to stop him. On the contrary…

'Belle…'

'Mmm….' Dreamily Belle opened her eyes at the same time as she snuggled deeper into Luc's arms.

'You know what's going to happen if we stay here like this, don't you?' Luc warned her.

'No,' Belle fibbed untruthfully as she delicately nuzzled the deliciously Luc-scented skin just below his jaw. 'But you could always show me,' she added helpfully, and encouragingly, just in case he hadn't quite got the message.

'Don't tempt me,' Luc told her throatily as he tasted the soft sweetness of her lips, deliberately lingering over them, teasing the warm outline of them with tiny little kisses.

'No, I won't tempt you,' Belle agreed obediently as she opened her mouth to the delicate probing of his tongue-tip.

Some time later, as he carried her to her bed...*their* bed...Luc reproved her, 'Didn't your mother ever tell you that it's wrong to tell lies?'

But Belle's only reply was a long, shuddering sigh of pleasure as he placed her naked body onto the bed and then covered it with his own.

'Oh, Luc... *Luc*... I've missed you so much,' she whispered to him as she held him tightly.

'Nowhere near as much as I've missed you,' he told her. 'Nowhere near...'

# CHAPTER FOUR

'PEOPLE are talking about us. I warned you that they would,' Belle told Luc, shaking her head reprovingly at him as he offered her the last of the petits fours. 'Your parents have been watching us very suspiciously for the last hour.'

'Mmm…' Luc responded. 'And so have yours.'

'Well, you've got to admit it *is* rather unusual for a divorced couple to be so…'

'Intimate with one another?' Luc suggested as she finally gave in and took the sweet he was lifting to her lips.

'*Friendly* with one another, I was going to say,' Belle corrected him sternly.

'Friendly!' Luc gave her an extremely wicked look. '*You* were rather more than friendly last night…'

Quickly Belle placed her fingertip to his lips.

'Don't you dare,' she warned him. 'Don't you *dare*.' But there was laughter and warmth in her eyes, rather than disapproval, and there was a matching warmth in Luc's.

'Darling…what on earth is going on? Luc's mother has just asked me how long you and Luc have been back on speaking terms, and I must say…'

'We decided it was time we put aside our differences,' Belle told her mother calmly, half an hour later.

'Well, yes…that's very sensible, darling, but I must say…'

'Carol wants you, Mum,' Belle warned her mother as she saw her elder sister frantically beckoning to their mother, smiling to herself as she quickly escaped from her parent's anxious questions. There was no doubt about it, she and Luc *had* created quite a stir. She could see the open speculation in people's eyes as they watched them. Only Joy, the bride, seemed oblivious to the undercurrents and speculation sweeping through the room.

'Aunt Belle, there you are. I just wanted to tell you again how grateful Andy and I are to you and Luc for your wonderful wedding present. I never expected…'

'You like it, then?' Belle asked her niece with a smile.

'Like it? We are over the moon. I never…I didn't even know you knew I wanted…'

'Your mother happened to mention that you'd seen it and fallen in love with it,' Belle informed her niece fondly.

'Yes. I had…*we* had. But for you and Luc…' She stopped and fell silent as Belle raised a quizzical eyebrow.

'Well, I suppose in a way it made sense for the two of you to give us a *joint* present,' Joy acknowledged breezily. 'After all you were once… Well, anyway, we're both thrilled with it. 'I'd always loved the one that you and Luc—' She stopped awkwardly. 'Oh, dear!'

'It's all right, darling, I fully understand what you're trying to say,' Belle reassured her.

'Oh, Andy,' Joy exclaimed thankfully as her new husband walked up. 'I was just telling Aunt Belle how thrilled we are with the present she and Luc gave us…'

'The bed? Too true. Joy had been dragging me over to that shop virtually every week.'

'I was so upset when the shop told me that it had been sold, even though I knew *we* couldn't afford it, and then when Luc came round and told me…'

'What was all that about?' Luc asked Belle, arriving back at their table as the bridal couple moved on to talk to some of their other wedding guests.

Whilst he handed Belle the drink he had gone to fetch for her she explained.

'They were thanking me...*us*...for their wedding present.'

'The bed?'

'The bed,' Belle agreed.

As he bent towards her Luc murmured provocatively, 'Well, if they get as much...pleasure out of using it as we have recently done ours...'

'Luc,' Bell warned him, and then added dryly, 'And you certainly weren't saying that when we divorced seven years ago.'

'That was then. I've come to see that shop-bought bed in a different light since then,' Luc told her suavely. 'A *very* different light...especially since you've bought those new curtains for the cottage. What was wrong with the old ones?'

'They were looking worn and tired. They were the same ones I put up before we divorced...'

'They reminded me of you,' Luc told her tenderly. 'That's why I kept them...'

'Watch out, here comes your mother,' Belle warned him.

'Luc…and Belle. You're looking wonderful, my dear…'

As she bent to kiss her ex-mother-in-law, Belle acknowledged that she had always got on well with Luc's mother, even if originally she had been a little in awe of her.

'What's this about you both giving Joy and Andrew a bed? And from the same place where— I should have thought…but then…'

'We've decided the time has come to forgive the bed its sins,' Luc told his mother mock gravely. 'After all, it wasn't entirely to blame.'

'Oh, Luc…if you're going to be flippant. I simply meant that I thought it was rather odd you should have chosen to give them something that wasn't even on their wedding list…and to give it to them jointly.'

'We decided that we could give them something a little more substantial if we combined our resources,' Belle told her gently.

'Well, yes, of course. But people do keep asking questions.'

'Perhaps we made the wrong decision,' Belle suggested.

There was a small, intimate pause, and then Luc responded obliquely, 'Oh, I don't think so.'

Belle remembered them making the decision to buy the bed, and the phone call which pre-dated it…

'Belle, I've had an idea…'

As she cradled the telephone receiver Belle felt a small frisson of pleasure begin to curl through her body. She had been away on business for three days, and it had been heaven to come home to find Luc's messages on her answering machine. And now here he was, ringing her to welcome her home.

'Mmm…?'

'About the wedding present…'

'Mmm…?'

'You did say you were coming home to house-sit for your parents this weekend, didn't you?'

'Mmm…'

'Well…'

When he'd finished telling her his idea, she exclaimed, 'You're saying that we should buy them a *bed*? Like the one we…I… It wasn't on their list.'

'No, I know, but Andy let slip that Joy would love to have one.'

'Well, yes, but, Luc! You don't think it would be tempting history to repeat itself, do you…?'

There was a small pause before Luc replied, 'Don't be silly. Besides, I thought we'd agreed.'

'It will cause talk—you know that, don't you? You and I giving them a joint gift.'

'I don't mind—let them talk,' Luc told her softly, adding persuasively, 'Andy says Joy's set her heart on the bed. It would be a wonderful surprise for Joy if we gave it to them. Andy's promised to keep it a secret from her.'

'Well, yes, I know what you're saying, and it would be lovely to surprise Joy with it.' Belle gave in.

'Yes, it would,' Luc agreed, and then asked her softly, 'What time this weekend are you expecting to arrive?'

'Belle, it's Carol. Look, I was wondering, since you're in Cambridgeshire for the next week, if you'd like to come round and have supper with us on Saturday evening. I'm not sure what time you're due to arrive, but I know that Mum and Dad are planning to leave for the airport at two in the afternoon. It would give us a chance to talk. I've been so busy with the wedding arrangements—'

'Carol, I have to go,' Belle interrupted her sister firmly. 'I'd love to see you whilst I'm down at Mum and Dad's house-sitting, but I'm afraid that Saturday night is going to be out.'

Deliberately she didn't offer any further explanation, swiftly ending the call before her sister could question her any further. There was no way she was going to tell Carol that the reason she couldn't accept her invitation was because she had already accepted an earlier one—from Luc.

And fortunately her sister was too preoccupied to question the deeply unusual circumstances of Belle and Luc giving Joy and Andy a joint wedding present.

From the sitting room window of her parents' house, Belle could see a car pulling into the drive. She drew in a sharp breath as she saw Luc climbing out of it and walking towards the front door.

'What are you doing here?' she demanded as she opened the door to him. 'You said you'd pick me up at eight o'clock tonight…'

'I know, but I couldn't wait any longer to see you,' Luc confessed as she let him in. 'Oh, Belle…'

Not since they had been a courting couple had they behaved like this, Belle acknowledged as Luc barely waited until he had closed the front door behind them to take her hungrily in his arms and kiss her with a passion which she admitted she had no difficulty whatsoever in matching.

'It's less than a week since you saw me,' Belle managed to find the logic to remind him when she was finally able to talk.

'A lifetime,' Luc told her mock solemnly, his tone belying the look of sparkling humour in his eyes.

This was a side of him she had never truly appreciated in the past, Belle acknowledged, as she shared his laughter, his sense of fun and teasing good humour. Perhaps because she had taken herself so seriously in those days, she had never allowed herself to appreciate it, but, as she was now discovering, shared laughter was a very, very potent aphrodisiac.

'Carol rang the other day. She wanted me to have dinner with *them* this evening.'

'What did you tell her?' Luc asked as he followed her into her parents' kitchen.

'I said that I'd got a prior engagement,' Belle informed him wryly.

'A prior *engagement*…mmm…'

There was no mistaking the way Luc reinforced the word 'engagement', and followed it with a meaningful look at her left hand.

'Luc, honestly!' Belle reproved him. 'What on earth would people think if they could see us…hear you…?'

'I don't care what other people think…only

what *you* think…what *you* feel,' Luc told her extravagantly.

'Oh, Luc…' A little shakily Belle went into his arms. 'Are we right to be behaving like this? We made a mistake once…'

'Look, we promised ourselves that we wouldn't question what was happening, that we'd just take things…and each other…on trust,' Luc reminded her.

'Yes, I know,' she admitted. 'It's just… Mmm… Luc, someone might see us,' she protested half-heartedly as he started to kiss her.

'Mmm…but at least this time it won't be your father,' Luc responded reminiscently. 'Remember that evening when he came down?'

'Mmm…he hadn't realised that you'd come in with me, and he walked into the kitchen, where I'd gone to make us both a cup of coffee…'

'And I'd followed you to help you.'

'Oh, that was what you were doing, was it?' Belle asked darkly.

'Well, at least this time there's no chance of your father walking in,' Luc commented, taking her back in his arms.

Several bliss-filled seconds later, Belle was just snuggling deeper into his embrace when the back door suddenly opened.

'Belle, it's me, Jane…' she heard her mother's friend and neighbour calling out cheerfully.

Any hopes that she and Luc had managed to spring apart without being seen were squashed when she heard Jane's voice change completely as she started to apologise in a flustered voice. 'Oh, dear, I'm sorry, I hadn't realised…' And then it changed again as she recognised Luc. 'Luc… But what…?'

'Luc called round to see Mum and Dad,' Belle fabricated quickly. 'He hadn't realised that they'd gone away.' Heavens, it was amazing how very creative one could be with the truth when the need arose, and she wasn't even blushing.

'Oh, I see…'

Uncertainly she looked from Belle to Luc, and then back again.

'How's your eye now, Belle?' Luc asked solicitously. 'She'd got an eyelash in it,' he told Jane straight-faced.

'Oh…I see… Well, I only called round to say hello,' Jane explained. 'Er…I'll er…leave you to it…'

'Now the whole neighbourhood is going to know that you were here,' Belle groaned after she had gone. 'Oh, Luc…'

'Oh, Belle…'

'Now what are you doing?' she demanded a little breathlessly as he took her back in his arms.

'Looking for that eyelash,' Luc told her.

'I just hope that Jane hasn't seen us driving away together,' Belle worried half an hour later as Luc backed his car out of her parents' drive.

'We've got a perfectly legitimate excuse for being seen together. We're buying Joy and Andy a joint wedding present—remember?'

'Yes, I know that, but we're not doing that now, are we?'

'No, we're not doing it now,' Luc agreed urbanely.

'So where *are* we going?' Belle asked him curiously ten minutes later. 'It's too early for dinner and…'

'Wait and see.'

As they passed the country church where her niece was to be married, Belle leant forward in her seat.

'Does it bring back memories?' Luc asked her.

'Yes,' Belle admitted.

They had been married there themselves, and her eyes blurred briefly with emotional tears as she remembered how deliriously happy she had been, how filled with excitement mingled with awe at the thought of marrying Luc.

Not that she had originally wanted a big white wedding with all the trimmings. She had wanted something far quieter and more intimate.

It had been Luc who had persuaded her otherwise, pointing out to her that the vows they made to one another would be just as precious no matter where they made them, and that it would be unfair of them to exclude their families from the occasion.

'You wanted to be married somewhere private and out in the open air—remember?'

'Yes, I do,' Belle agreed, her voice a little husky with emotion at the way he had picked up on her own thoughts. 'An island, or the top of a hill... I wanted our marriage to be different, special...romantic, a private memory we could cherish for ever...'

'I know.'

'Instead it was a full family affair with me in a dress like a meringue and eight bridesmaids.'

'You looked beautiful.'

'You could barely get close enough to kiss me after the vicar had said you could because of the width of my dress hoops. Remember?'

Luc started to laugh.

'It wasn't funny,' Belle protested indignantly. 'A bride whose groom can't kiss her is no laughing matter.'

'I wasn't laughing at that,' Luc told her. 'I was just remembering the panic we had when no one could find little Timmy and then he crawled out from underneath your skirt.'

Belle laughed too.

'Yes, he'd been under the table whilst I was talking to his parents and he'd crawled under my hoops without any of us noticing.'

Silently they exchanged reminiscent looks, and then out of the corner of her eye Belle saw a familiar signpost.

'You're taking me home?' she asked Luc incredulously, not realising until it was too late just how betraying her choice of words had been.

'I'm taking you home,' Luc agreed huskily.

This time the silence between them was deeper, closer, and potentially tense with unspoken emotion. Belle could feel her heart starting to beat far too fast as they drove through the village and Luc took the narrow country lane that led to the house they had bought together.

Belle had fallen in love with it at first sight, and the feelings that swamped her as they rounded the bend and she saw the house through its framing protective canopy of trees made her press her lips firmly together to stop her chin from wobbling and trembling. They had bought

this house with such love and she had left it in so
much pain that she could hardly bear to
remember just how she had felt.

'It hasn't changed,' Belle whispered as Luc
stopped the car.

Originally two separate farmworkers' cottages,
the pair had been knocked through into one when
they had bought it, and the whole building carefully renovated.

It was surrounded by a large garden overlook-
ing the lane at the front and running down to a
stream at the rear. Inside the front door was a long,
narrow stone-flagged hallway and a flight of steep
stairs. The stone mullioned windows gave the
house character and an air of timelessness.

'Oh, you've still got the same curtains,' was
the only thing she could think of to say as Luc
helped her out of the car.

She had bought the material on impulse one wet
afternoon when Luc had been studying and she
had driven into Cambridge to do some shopping.

She had found the heavy damask fabric by
accident on a market stall. It had come originally
from one of the colleges, the stall owner had told
her.

Uncertainly Belle had fingered the rich heavy
fabric. Even at the stall holder's price it was still

horribly expensive, but it was also perfect for the house.

She reminded herself that only the previous week she and Luc had rowed about money, and in retaliation for his claim that their expenses were far too high she had immediately accused him of spending far too much on the books he had claimed he needed to study.

'I thought that's what college libraries were for,' she had told him scornfully, still smarting from his reference to the fact that she had spent more on a pair of luxury tights then he had done on a whole week's lunches.

'It is, but they don't carry a set of these,' Luc had countered quietly.

So she had walked determinedly away from the stall, only to walk back again ten minutes later, closing her eyes as she told the woman she would have the fabric.

She had made the curtains herself. How could she preach economy to Luc and then pay someone else to make them?

'They're beautiful,' Luc had told her quietly once they were hung, but the lack of genuine enthusiasm in his voice had hurt and angered her.

If she wanted to spend the money she had worked so hard to earn on expensive curtains, then she had every right to do so. And she had told him so.

Remembering the incident now, Belle winced at her own careless disregard of Luc's feelings, her lack of wisdom and foresight.

'The shop has sent me a brochure with photographs of the different styles of beds they do,' Luc explained as he unlocked the front door and ushered Belle in in front of him. 'Since they don't carry a stock of each design, I thought you might want to look at it.'

'Do they still do our bed?'

'"Our" bed?' Luc gave her a slow, teasing smile. 'It's *my* bed now—remember? The removal men took the one I made when you moved out. Of course it's not too late for us to—'

'No, no, I don't want—I'm keeping the bed I've got,' Belle told him quickly, and then added a little defensively, 'I like it, I'm used to it—it's…'

It's a tiny bit of you, she could have said.

Belle shot Luc a slightly self-conscious look, but he was already ushering her towards the drawing room.

'Come and sit down. I'll make us both a cup of tea and then you can look at the brochure.'

The sitting room was just as she had left it. The covers on the sofas a little faded, perhaps, and the rust carpet's original colour softened by the sun, but the classic timelessness of the furniture Belle had chosen because the house had demanded it had stood the passage of time very well, she acknowledged.

Luc might not have changed anything, but she could see that the room had been repainted at some stage and its surfaces were dust-free and well polished.

'Sorry about the delay,' he apologised ten minutes later, when he reappeared with their tea and the catalogue. 'I couldn't find this. Mrs Leyton, who comes in from the village to clean for me a couple of times a week, had "tidied" it away.'

Being in the house which had once been her home, the home she had once shared with Luc, who was here beside her, whose home it still was, was causing her to feel so many conflicting emotions that Belle could barely concentrate on the brochure he was showing her.

Certainly the company had extended its original small range of furniture, and the four-poster beds they had added to their list were works of art—and had she been looking for a new bed—

But they weren't looking for a bed for the master bedroom here; they were looking for one for Joy and Andy. And since they already knew exactly which one they wanted...

'I really ought to get back,' Belle told Luc hurriedly, closing the brochure. 'But first I need to go upstairs and wash my hands…'

One of the drawbacks to the house had been the fact that it had not possessed a downstairs cloakroom. They had had plans to add one at the same time as they added an extra bedroom suite. Confidently Belle made her way upstairs whilst Luc carried their tea things back to the kitchen.

Up here, too, nothing seemed to have changed. The dried flowers she had arranged were gone from the deep window on the landing, but the curtains were the same, and… On her way to the bathroom she suddenly paused, stopped, and then retraced her steps.

The door to the master bedroom was closed. Very gently she turned the handle and then stepped inside.

It was like stepping back in time to another world. Once inside the bedroom she had shared with Luc the memories came flooding back with such force that she had to cling to the door for support. It was in this room that they had loved, laughed and fought. Belle could hardly bear now to think of the sacrilege it had been to fight in a room which should have known only the intimate content of their love.

Shakily she let go of the door and walked over to the bed, her hand trembling as she automatically smoothed the creases out of Luc's side of the duvet.

Luc's side...

Unwanted and unheralded the tears came hot and fast, a silent glissade of pain and regret. Her body shook with the force of her sobs, but still she didn't make a sound.

'Belle?'

Shocked, she stiffened her body in rejection of the warmth of Luc's arms. She hadn't heard him come in, didn't want him to see her like this.

'You're crying,' he told her, begging rawly as he turned her round to face him, 'Don't...please, don't.'

'Oh, Luc, I feel so ashamed when I remember the things I did...the things I said,' Belle wept, unable to conceal what she was feeling. 'I was so thoughtless, so selfish...'

'No more thoughtless or selfish than I was stubborn and unreasonable,' Luc comforted her.

'It's all such a waste,' Belle cried heartbrokenly.

'Love is never wasted,' Luc told her softly. 'Just like it never dies...'

Belle looked up at him.

'It's not too late for us, Belle, we still have the future...*our* future...together—if we choose to take it...'

'What are you saying?' she whispered. 'We said that we wouldn't rush things or make promises, that we'd take each day as it comes…'

'I know, but I know as well that each day isn't going to be enough for me. I want all your days. All *our* days.'

'Remember Cheringham House?' he asked her obliquely.

Belle nodded her head. The stately Georgian property was owned by the local council and had been painstakingly renovated and opened to the public. She had always loved it, often coaxing Luc away from his studies to go round it with her.

'Under the new law, it's now been given permission to hold weddings. It has an island…'

'In the middle of the lake with a pretty mock-Gothic temple… Yes, I know,' Belle agreed.

And then, as she looked at him, she breathed, 'Oh, Luc, we couldn't…could we?'

Ten minutes later, when she had finally extracted herself from his arms, she reminded him, 'We're supposed to be going out to dinner, remember?'

'I've got a better idea,' Luc told her masterfully. 'Why don't we eat here…?'

'Here?'

Belle looked at him.

'What are we going to eat?' she asked him shakily.

'I know what I want to eat,' Luc responded sensually. 'All right, all right,' he acknowledged as he fielded the look she gave him. 'Let's go down and see what we can find in the freezer.'

'Mmm…champagne and lobster. You really are spoiling me,' Belle told Luc contentedly as she licked her fingers.

'Well, I have to admit it was a lucky find. I'd forgotten all about the lobster. It was a present…'

'From one of your students?' Belle asked a little possessively, a warning glint in her eyes.

Luc laughed.

'No, from my mother, as it happens.'

Belle allowed herself to relax. His mother was a wonderful cook, and loved nothing better than passing on the results of her skills to her friends and family.

'Mmm…that was wonderful,' Belle declared, stretching sensuously.

'Mmm…wonderful,' Luc agreed, reaching across to slide his hand into the tempting vee of flesh exposed by the borrowed shirt she was wearing and bending his head to kiss her.

'Just think,' he murmured as he covered her

mouth with his, 'if we bought a four-poster, we could close the curtains and eat in bed in true Tudor fashion.'

'Throwing the bones out for the dogs and serfs, you mean?' Belle teased back, wrinkling her nose as she disagreed. 'Yuck, I don't think so. Although I must admit the idea of a four-poster does have a certain amount of appeal…'

'Mmm…although I have to say that there is something deliciously sensual about the way the light from the window touches your skin which I couldn't enjoy through closed curtains.'

'Luc…' Belle reproved unsteadily as he gently pushed his shirt back off her shoulders, exposing her breasts to the early evening sunlight streaming in through the windows, and then moved back to enjoy the results of his handiwork.

'Your skin looks as though it's been sprinkled with gold dust,' he told her softly. 'You have the most beautiful skin, Belle, the most beautiful body…'

'I'm thirty-four,' Belle protested, but in truth she thought that Luc's body looked even more sensually exciting now than it had done when they were younger. Perhaps Luc was right in what he had said to her earlier, that it took pain and loss and despair to make one appreciate love properly.

Well, she had certainly experienced all of those.
They both had.

She trembled a little with excited anticipation
as Luc's hands cupped her breasts. Her body was
so intensely responsive to him it frightened her a
little.

He kissed her throat and then her nipples, his
eyes darkening as he looked back into her face.

'I don't know how I managed to live without
you,' he told her rawly, and then added, 'But it
wasn't really living; it was simply existing.'

His mouth returned to her breasts, teasing their
hard crests. Belle moaned eagerly beneath her
breath and reached for him. Her need for him
overwhelmed her, urgent, immediate and hotly
demanding. The feel of his weight against her
body, between her thighs, made her shudder
wildly. Her hands clasped his back, her nails
pressed hard against his skin as she clung passion-
ately to him. She cried out as he entered her, a
wild, elemental cry of love and need mingled with
pain and regret for all that they had lost, all that
she had thrown away, and then the past was forgotten, the future just a shadowy vision, the only
thing that mattered the thrusting movement of his
body within hers.

Luc cried out fiercely against her as his own

need peaked and her body exploded into a frantic spiral of orgasmic pleasure.

Damp, panting, her heart still racing, Belle looked up into his eyes.

'Great-Aunt Alice could have an awful lot to answer for,' she warned him meaningfully. 'This wasn't something I'd planned for…'

'All the more reason to take that trip to Cheringham House just as soon as we can, then,' Luc responded.

'I might not—' Belle began, but Luc shook his head, and then bent it and kissed her tenderly.

'With or without child, I want you back in my life, Belle.' Belle snuggled closer to him and then tensed.

'Luc, I don't want to have to tell anyone about us…not yet…it's too soon. What we have between us is too…precious. I…'

'I understand,' Luc confirmed as he kissed her again.

'Belle.'

Belle gave Luc an answering smile as he called her name and cut a swathe through the busy fellow wedding guests to reach her side.

'What happened?' he asked her quietly, adding with a rueful look, 'I was just beginning to wonder if I ought to send my mother on a search party to the Ladies for you.'

'It's just as well that you didn't,' Belle whispered, glancing warningly at where his hand rested, just a little too possessively and potentially betrayingly on her arm. 'Body language, Luc,' she reminded him under her breath. 'People are watching us.'

'Mmm…what do you mean, just as well I didn't?' Luc demanded, ignoring the second part of her comment.

'I never actually got as far as the cloakroom,' Belle informed him as they were caught up in the throng of people moving excitedly towards the exit so that they could watch the bride and groom leave.

'Why, what happened?' Luc asked her anxiously.

'My mobile started to ring,' Belle answered him, 'and once I realised who was calling I decided that it might be an idea to make sure I took the call in private. So I went out to the car.'

'In private?' Luc started to frown.

'Look over there at Luc and Belle,' Luc's mother sighed disappointedly at her husband as she caught sight of her son's frowning face.

'Just when I thought that the pair of them seemed to be getting on so well. I suppose I should have known it was too good to be true. And to think I'd actually begun to hope...' She shook her head ruefully. 'They always seemed so right for one another, and I can't help wishing...'

'Leave them to lead their own lives,' her husband advised her gently.

'In private,' Luc repeated with concern.

'Mmm...' Belle responded dreamily.

Belle's face was slightly flushed and Luc could almost feel the excitement bubbling up inside her. Her eyes, when he looked down into them, shone with barely concealed happiness. So much so that he could almost feel it radiating from her. She looked, Luc decided wryly, buoyed up with a secret—and with love.

'It must have been a very special call—and a very special caller.' Luc couldn't resist challenging her.

Belle's smile deepened, and so did her pretty pink colour.

'It was,' she admitted candidly.

'Belle, quick. She's leaving. Here...'

A handful of rose petals were pushed into Belle's hand by her mother, to shower onto the bride. Obediently, Belle turned her attention away from Luc and towards her niece and her new husband.

'Belle looks wonderful, doesn't she?' one of Belle's female cousins commented to another.

'Positively glowing…'

Belle, who had overheard their comment, waited until they were out of earshot before turning to Luc and remarking in a very, very soft whisper, 'Positively *blooming* might have been a more *appropriate* description—under the circumstances. Doubly so, in view of the fact…' She added mock coyly.

She stopped and waited for the penny to drop.

'My call was from the doctor's surgery,' she added helpfully, her own face breaking into a wide grin of excited happiness as she saw the enlightenment dawn in Luc's eyes.

'It's quite definitely twins,' she told him breathlessly.

'Twins… Two babies…' Luc gazed at her in adoring awe.

'Yes, twins does mean two babies,' Belle agreed teasingly, tongue in cheek.

She had had her suspicions for a while that she might be pregnant—she had even gone out and bought herself a home pregnancy test. But Luc had been away at the time, and in the end, she had wanted him to be there to share the moment with her. After all, he had been there—very much there—when their baby had been conceived, and they had agreed that this time round they were going to share their lives as true partners, true lovers.

Luc had been with her when she had first been told that she might be carrying twins, and today's phone call was the formal confirmation of the news they had already unofficially been given.

'Luc—Luc, stop it,' Belle protested as Luc suddenly wrapped her in his arms and gazed deeply into her eyes before starting to kiss her.

'Luc, people are watching us,' Belle protested huskily beneath his mouth. 'Luc… Luc… Mmm… Mmm…'

'Let them watch,' Luc whispered back hoarsely.

Around them Belle could hear the astonished whispers of the other guests as they turned away from the departing bridal car to stare at Belle and Luc.

'I think we'd better tell them, don't you?' Luc whispered lovingly. 'Otherwise, if we don't…'

His hand covered her still flat stomach protectively, and even though she knew technically it was impossible as yet Belle could have sworn the two beings they had created with their love were kicking their assent to their father's suggestion.

'Well, they're going to have to know some time,' Belle agreed philosophically as she glanced down at her body. 'But a lot of them might not approve,' she warned him. 'After all, it's not exactly conventional.'

'We have the right to live our lives the way we want to live them, unconventional or not,' Luc argued softly.

And then, still holding her in the protective circle of his arm, he cleared his throat and began, 'Ladies and gentlemen, family and friends. Belle and I have an announcement to make.'

As he looked down at her, Belle looked back up at him, all the love she felt for him showing clearly in her eyes. A shaft of light touched the gold of the new wedding ring she had just removed from her purse and slipped onto her wedding finger—they had had it made from the gold of her old ring and Luc's, a symbolic fusing of the old to create new in a bond that could never be broken.

Her sister saw it first, pre-empting Luc's announcement by screaming excitedly,

'Belle, you're married—you and Luc have re-married! Oh, how could you, without saying anything. Oh, Belle…Luc… Oh, this is so wonderful…'

'Wonderful,' Luc echoed as he raised Belle's hand to his mouth and gently kissed her fingers.

Through the excited hubbub that followed, Belle could hear her great-aunt Alice saying quite clearly to her mother, 'There you are, Mary, I knew I was right. They *are* married…'

As their relatives pressed happily around them, Belle could feel the joy bubbling up inside her.

Oh yes, they were married—had remarried. In a small, perfect, private ceremony on the island on the lake at Cheringham House, two weeks ago.

She had wanted to keep it a secret for just a little longer but… She patted her stomach tenderly.

Some events had a way of precipitating their own celebrations.

Above the heads of their excited audience Luc mouthed softly to her, I love you—and them.

Blissfully Belle returned his smile. One day—not this time, perhaps, but one day—they would have a little girl, and when they did, when they did, she rather thought they might call her Alice.